peg + cat

THE PUDDLE

JENNIFER OXLEY
+ BILLY ARONSON

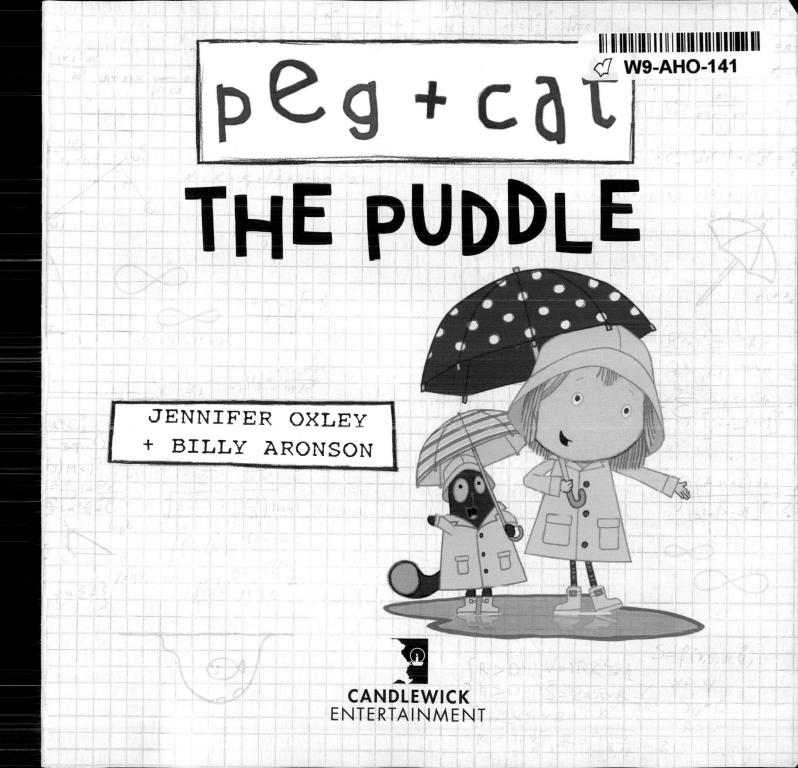

CANDLEWICK
ENTERTAINMENT

It was raining, and weatherman Ramone didn't like it.

"It's not the kind of day you want to spend in the park," he said.

It was raining, and Peg and Cat liked it very much!
For them, it was the perfect day to go to the park.

They were all set, with their rain boots,
raincoats, rain hats, and umbrellas.

3 + 1 = 4

"Good news!" said Ramone. "The rain's going to stop soon. The sun will come out."

4 + 1 = 5

"Hurry!" said Peg. "We have to play in these puddles before they dry up!"

5 + 1 = 6

Peg jumped into a puddle.

"WOO-HOO!"

Cat dipped a toe in a
puddle. "Huh."

6 + 1 = 7

Peg jumped into a bigger puddle.
"HO YEAH! YA HAA! WHEEE!"

Cat dipped a toe in
another puddle. "Huh."

7 + 1 = 8

"What's wrong, Cat?" asked Peg.

"I'm worried, Peg," said Cat. "This puddle might be too . . ." Cat held out his paws, one below the other.

8 + 1 = 9

"Deep?" said Peg.

"What does deep mean?" asked Cat.

"Deep means how far down something goes,"
Peg explained.

9+1=10

"Really deep puddles make me nervous," said Cat.
"If I jump in, I'll get my tail wet!"

"But you can't tell how deep a puddle is just by
looking at it," said Peg.

"So I can't tell which puddles to play in," said Cat.

"Cat has a DEEP PROBLEM!" said Ramone.

Cat sighed and leaned against his umbrella.

12+1=13

"That's it, you umbrella-leaning genius!" said Peg.
"We can use the stripes on your umbrella to measure
how deep the puddle is!"

Peg used the umbrella to measure up from the ground to Cat's tail. "One, two, three stripes," she said. "So if a puddle is three stripes deep, your tail won't get wet!"

14+1=15

Cat dipped the umbrella into the puddle until it reached the bottom.

Then he took the umbrella out and counted the wet stripes. "One, two, three, four stripes. This puddle is too deep for me," he said.

"Come on, Cat," said Peg. "We'll find you puddles
that aren't very deep so you can jump right in!"

As Peg and Cat measured and splashed,
they sang and danced.

"We're measuring in the rain!
Just measuring in the rain!"
"This puddle's two stripes deep,
so I'm splashing again!"
"These markings are plain.
Use your umbrella and your brain!
And measure, just measure in the rain!"

18 + 1 = 19

"Thanks to my umbrella with measuring stripes," said Cat, "my problem is solved!"

Cat dipped his umbrella into another puddle. "One, two, three stripes. Not too deep!"

"Wait," said Peg. "I think we should stop and have a moment of reflection."

20+1=21

Peg and Cat looked at their reflections in the puddle.
"That was nice," said Cat. "Now can we get back to--"
"You bet we can!" said Peg.

21+1=22

SPLASH!

This book is based on the TV series *Peg + Cat*.
Peg + Cat is produced by The Fred Rogers Company.
Created by Jennifer Oxley and Billy Aronson.
The Puddle is based on a television script, *The Umbrella Problem*,
by Stacey Greenberger and background art by Erica Kepler.
Art assets assembled by Sarika Matthew.
The PBS KIDS logo is a registered mark of the
Public Broadcasting Service and is used with permission.

pbskids.org/peg

First edition 2019

Library of Congress Catalog Card Number pending
ISBN 978-1-5362-0698-2

18 19 20 21 22 23 APS 10 9 8 7 6 5 4 3 2 1

Printed in Humen, Dongguan, China

This book was typeset in OPTITypewriter.
The illustrations were created digitally.

Candlewick Entertainment
an imprint of Candlewick Press
99 Dover Street
Somerville, Massachusetts 02144

visit us at www.candlewick.com